Fairies of
Blossom Bakery

Butterfly

and the

Birthday Surprise

Picture Corgi

Some fluttery fun for Lara Flew, hugs – M.A.
To Scarlet, with thanks - K.H-J.

FAIRIES OF BLOSSOM BAKERY: BUTTERFLY AND THE BIRTHDAY SURPRISE A PICTURE CORGI BOOK 978 0 552 56903 3 Published in Great Britain by Picture Corgi, an imprint of Random House Children's Publishers UK A Random House Group Company This edition published 2014 1 3 5 7 9 10 8 6 4 2 Copyright © Random House Children's Publishers UK, 2014 Written by Mandy Archer Illustrated by Kirsteen Harris-Jones The right of Mandy Archer and Kirsteen Harris-Jones to be identified as the author and illustrator of this work has been asserted in accordance with the Copyright, Designs and Patents Act 1988. All rights reserved. Picture Corgi Books are published by Random House Children's Publishers UK, 61–63 Uxbridge Road, London W5 5SA www.randomhousechildrens.co.uk www.randomhouse.co.uk Addresses for companies within The Random House Group Limited can be found at: www.randomhouse.co.uk/offices.htm THE RANDOM HOUSE GROUP Limited Reg. No. 954009 A CIP catalogue record for this book is available from the British Library. Printed in China

Fairies of Blossom Bakery

Cupcake

Butterfly

Over the hills in a land of sweetness,
little fairies bake and play.
Would you like to peep at their secret,
scrumptious world?

Make a wish, then step
into the magic of Fairycake Kingdom
and meet the fairies…

Cookie

Plum

Sparkle

Button

Trrrriing!

Butterfly the fairy popped on her oven gloves and opened the oven. Inside, a neat stack of sweet pancakes was nicely warming.

"My favourite breakfast!" she declared happily. "Now, there's only a week until my birthday and still so much to do."

This year, Butterfly wanted to celebrate with a fabulous party. She flipped open her fairy catalogue and gazed longingly at the daffodil-yellow gown with the twinkly net skirt she'd ordered. "It's the prettiest party frock ever!" she sighed. "I can't wait to wear it."

Butterfly fluttered over to the Blossom Bakery and Café to visit Cupcake.
Every branch of the fine old tree was draped in a mist of frothy pink flowers. Elves and fairies sat under the canopy of petals, chattering in the sunshine. Cookie, Button, Sparkle and Plum looked up and waved.
"Morning!" trilled Sparkle. "Isn't the blossom heavenly today?"

Butterfly nodded, before rushing straight up to the café counter.

"Hello!" Cupcake smiled. "Would you like a milkshake?"

Butterfly nodded, then crossed her fingers hopefully. "I have something special to ask," she said. "Would I be able to hold a party at the bakery next week? It's my birthday!"

Cupcake agreed at once – fairies adore parties! Butterfly skipped over to share the news with her friends. They clapped their hands in excitement.

"How delightful!" cried Plum. "I can't wait!"

"There'll be dancing and sweet things to eat," said Butterfly, as they walked outside. "I've got masses to do!"

"You can't do everything," insisted Cookie. "Not when we're here to help."

"That's what friends are for," chipped in Cupcake.

Butterfly beamed. She thought they'd never ask! The birthday fairy tapped her wand. Five tiny lists appeared.

Cupcake
Make bunting
Party nibbles

Cookie
Posies for the tables
Buy fairy fizz

Button
Streamers and glitter
Party bags

Sparkle
Deliver invites
Music

Plum
Blow up balloons
Party games

The next day at the Fairy Academy, Madame Drizzle taught the fairies
how to open up the flowers ready for spring.

"Tap the daffodil with your wand," she instructed, "and it bursts into colour!"

"I want yellow party decorations," whispered Butterfly, "to match my outfit."

"You've really thought of everything - but what about surprises?" said Plum.

Butterfly shook her head firmly. Every detail had to be party-perfect.

As soon as the bell rang, the fairies buckled up their satchels.

"Better hurry," chimed Button. "Cupcake is waiting outside."

Sparkle nodded. She had lots of invites to deliver!

"I'll catch up with you later," called Butterfly, plucking the top invite from the pile. "I want to give this to Madame Drizzle."

Cupcake had fluttered along to the academy steps, her eyes twinkling with excitement. She believed that every party needed at least one special surprise . . .

"Let's make a birthday cake for Butterfly," she whispered. "It can be our secret."

Plum, Sparkle, Cookie and Button dissolved into a delighted peal of fairy giggles.

"Stand back, please. Coming through!"

The fairies gasped. Butterfly came staggering out of the lobby carrying an ENORMOUS cake box! She proudly lifted the lid.

"Do you like my birthday cake?" she said. "Madame Drizzle helped me bake it!"

The fairies peered into the box. The cake was fancy, frilly and fabulous – just like Butterfly.

"It looks beautiful," agreed Cupcake sadly.

The party got closer and closer. Butterfly got busier and busier.

On the day before her birthday, she started with a magical manicure at the Snail Nail Bar.

Then she swooshed to Bubbles Hair Salon for a shampoo and style.

Next she flitted to Acorn Post Office to pick up her new party outfit.

Cupcake and her friends were over at the Elf Market trying to buy a birthday present, when Butterfly suddenly appeared.

"You can't stop here," she insisted, shooing the fairies on their way. "The bakery needs decorating!"

"The market closes in five minutes," said Pippin.

Plum sighed. Now they couldn't even surprise Butterfly with a special gift!

Butterfly got ready to work her magic on Blossom Bakery. There was bunting to drape, glitter to sprinkle and balloons to blow up!

"Can you make one more posy of daffodils, Cookie?" she called. "All the flowers need to be yellow to go with my colour scheme."

Each time Sparkle was sure they must be finished, Butterfly thought of something else to do.

"There!" declared Cupcake, when the lists were all ticked. "Is this party-perfect?"

Butterfly stopped to admire the decorated terrace. It looked enchanting. "We're ready, everyone," she said happily. "Thank you!"

It was now the fairies' bedtime. Butterfly's birthday was only hours away!

♫♪♫♪ "Happy birthday to you!" ♫♪♫♪

Butterfly sat up in bed. Was she dreaming?

The bedroom door clicked open. In a shimmering swirl of fairy dust, Cupcake, Sparkle, Button, Plum and Cookie all tumbled inside. Butterfly couldn't help but laugh!

"Time to celebrate!" said Plum, "we've all been longing to surprise you on your special day."

"We wanted to be the first fairies to see you," exclaimed Button.

"I made these," chipped in Sparkle, unwrapping a napkin full of delicious blueberry muffins. "They're still warm."

After their scrumptious breakfast, the fairies were about to set off home to get ready, but Butterfly had one last job for Cupcake.

"Please would you take my birthday cake over to the bakery?" she asked. "It's on the kitchen table."

Butterfly's birthday cake was heavy. Soon party guests began to pass her along the way.

"Oh bother!" she puffed, stopping to catch her breath.

Pippin cycled up beside her. "Need a hand?" he asked.

The kindly elf loaded the box on to his delivery bike and rang the bell.

"Please be careful!" cried Butterfly.

"Where have you been?" asked Button, when Butterfly finally made it to the party.

"No time to talk," said the fairy. "I need my dress!"

"You can't change now," Pippin told her. "Everybody's here."

Cupcake was very sorry about the mix-up. She undid the box and lifted out the cake.

It was a disaster! Butterfly's creation wasn't so fabulous any more. The frosting was bashed and the tiers were dented. Even the little fairy had been knocked off the top.

"My cake's ruined!" wailed Butterfly.

"It's not so bad," soothed Sparkle.

Butterfly didn't think things could get any worse, but then . . . *splish-splosh!* Silver raindrops pitter-pattered on to the party. The sprinkling turned into a shower, and the shower turned into a downpour. Pixies, fairies and gnomes scattered in every direction.

Butterfly's friends helped her indoors. The fairy stood forlornly in the bakery kitchen and burst into tears.

"Everyone's gone home," she sniffed. "It's a washout!"

"Why don't you put on your new dress now?" suggested Cupcake, lifting it out of the box. "That's still party-perfect."

"I suppose it might cheer me up," admitted Butterfly. The stunning dress was hard to resist. As soon as she'd fluttered back to her house to change, the fairies got to work. They had a birthday to rescue!

Cupcake brought over the soggy cake, then put on her pinny. Sparkle whipped up a fresh batch of frosting. Cookie picked some strawberries. A little piping here and a dusting of sugar there, and the cake was fairy-fabulous all over again! There was a rustling, then Butterfly appeared in her new dress. She looked divine.

The birthday fairy gasped. Her soggy cake had been transformed into a dainty strawberry sponge with butterfly wings! She made a fairy wish as she blew out the candles.

"I am sorry I was so bossy," said Butterfly. "Celebrating with special friends is the best present a fairy could wish for."

At that moment, the sun began to glitter through the rain showers. "Look outside," exclaimed Cookie. "There's a rainbow!"

Butterfly's heart filled with wonder. She could never have planned a party like this! Her best birthday ever was all thanks to the magic of fairy friends.

Butterfly's Fluttery Wings Cake

A lighter-than-air butterfly sponge cake for everyone to share.

Shopping list for one Fluttery Wings Cake

- 225g butter, plus a little extra for greasing
- 225g caster sugar
- 1 teaspoon vanilla extract
- 225g self-raising flour
- 2 teaspoons baking powder
- 4 eggs
- 250g mascarpone cheese
- 50g lemon curd
- punnet of fresh strawberries
- icing sugar for dusting

Always ask a grown-up to help you in the kitchen, especially when using the oven.

1. Ask a grown-up to pre-heat the oven to 180°C/350°F/Gas Mark 4. Grease the inside of two cake tins with the extra butter, then cut out a circle of baking parchment and line each one.

2. Tip the butter, caster sugar, vanilla, self-raising flour and baking powder into a large mixing bowl. Crack in the eggs, then beat the ingredients together. You can do this with a wooden spoon, but it is much easier if you can use a hand mixer.

3. Carefully share the mixture out between the two cake tins, then ask your grown-up to pop the tins in the oven to bake.

4. After 25 minutes, your cakes should be golden brown and beautifully risen. Ask your grown-up to turn them out on to a rack so that they can cool.

5. While the sponges are cooling, find another clean bowl. Measure out the lemon curd and mascarpone, then use a fork to blend them together. This will be the creamy filling that holds your cake together. Next ask your grown-up to help wash and slice the strawberries.

6. Look at your two sponge cakes carefully. Which one has risen the most? The sponge with the biggest dome in the middle should go on the top of your cake. Lay the flatter one on the bottom, spread over a layer of lemon cream and place some strawberries on the top.

7. Lay the deeper sponge on to the creamy layer, then carefully slice off the top of the dome. Spread more lemon cream into the hole left in the middle of the cake. Now cut the sliced top section in half and turn the pieces round. Gently balance them in the cream so that they look like wings. Add the rest of the strawberry pieces as decoration and dust over a sprinkling of icing sugar. Your fluttery butterfly is good enough to eat!

Fairy Tip:
Fairies always wash their hands before starting a new recipe!

Fairies of
Blossom Bakery

Did you enjoy your visit to the

Fairycake Kingdom?

Join the Fairies of Blossom Bakery in
some of their other adventures:

♥ Cupcake and the Princess Party

♥ Cookie and the Secret Sleepover

♥ Plum and the Winter Ball

♥ Sparkle and the Pixie Picnic

♥ Button and the Baking Disaster